This edition published by Parragon Books Ltd in 2015

Parragon Books Ltd
Chartist House
15–17 Trim Street
Bath BA1 1HA, UK
www.parragon.com

ISBN 978-1-4723-8580-2

Printed in Poland

Disney FAIRIES

TinkerBell
AND THE
LEGEND OF THE
NEVERBEAST

PaRragon

Bath • New York • Cologne • Melbourne • Delhi
Hong Kong • Shenzhen • Singapore • Amsterdam

On a night like any other in Pixie Hollow, Iridessa, a light-talent fairy, was gathering light beams. She didn't notice the mysterious green star – the fourth from the right – in the sky.

Nor did she notice when it began to move. It wasn't a star at all, but a comet. Ancient fairy lore, all but forgotten, revealed that the very same comet had come nearly a thousand years before.

The comet's light caught the attention of curious Tinker Bell. The light in the sky was unlike anything she'd ever seen.

Scribble, a reading-talent sparrowman, watched the comet through a telescope. He made notes on everything he saw. But still he wanted to know more.

The green light continued on, spilling into every dark corner and cave. And, deep down in the earth, something began to stir.

The next morning, Fawn, a fun-loving animal-talent fairy, greeted
Tinker Bell. The tinker-talent fairy had made a huge wagon for her.

"Just like you ordered," said Tink. "But what are you up to?"

Fawn took Tink inside her home and Tink was shocked by what
she saw. "You have a hawk!" gasped Tink. "Hawks eat fairies!"

"Adult hawks, yes," said Fawn. "But Hannah is technically a baby."

Fawn had found the bird and fixed her wing. "We have to get
Hannah out without causing widespread panic!" she announced.

Fawn and Tink put Hannah into the wagon and covered her with blueberries. They pulled the wagon through Pixie Hollow.

"What's with the berries?" Rosetta, a garden-talent fairy, asked.

"Oh, we're just taking them to the forest," said Fawn.

Rosetta offered to help move the berries by sprinkling pixie dust on them. The berries rose into the air and uncovered Hannah!

"HAWK!" screamed a fairy.

Startled, Hannah let out a loud screech!

The adult hawks heard Hannah's screech and flew in to help her.
They scared the forest animals and chased the fairies!

Luckily, the scout fairies – the protectors of Pixie Hollow – arrived.
They used ropes, spears and their speed to confuse the hawks and
chase them away.

The scouts turned to Hannah and covered her with a net.

"Let her go!" demanded Fawn.

Nyx, the leader of the scouts, scowled. "We'll handle this."

"Is everyone all right?" asked Queen Clarion. It wasn't the first time that Fawn had helped a dangerous animal.

The queen smiled at her. "You've always let your heart be your guide, but –"

"But I also need to listen with my head," said Fawn. "Next time, I promise, I will."

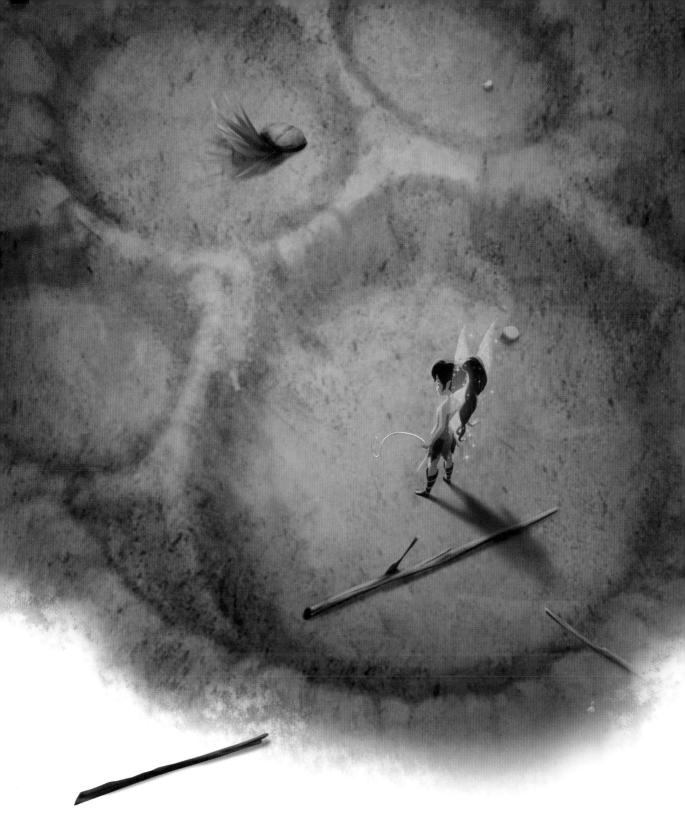

The following day, Fawn decided to be a model fairy and teach a group of bunnies to hop. In the middle of the class, she heard a loud, deep groan come from the forest.

"I should probably check that out," Fawn said. She followed a trail of broken branches to an odd clump of fur. Then Fawn realized she was standing in a gigantic paw print!

Fawn followed the paw prints to a clearing. The rocks and plants there were twisted, as if by a huge force. And right in the middle was a dark cave. Fawn cautiously peered inside, her heart racing.

"Come on," she told herself. "Listen to your head. Your heart gets you in trouble."

But Fawn just had to know what was inside.

Cautiously Fawn made her way to the bottom of the deep, jagged cave. What she found surprised even her: a huge animal unlike anything she'd ever seen!

"What are you?" she breathed.

The beast stood up. Fawn tried to keep her cool as she faced the enormous creature. Without warning, the beast let out a furious, ground-shaking, "ROOOOAAARRRR!"

Fawn decided to observe the animal from a distance.
She watched him pick up rocks and stack them in a pile.
Then, he stuck them together with snodgrass sap and spit.

The beast was limping. Fawn could see a thorn stuck
in his front paw. She had an idea.

Using a rope, she hung a rock from a tree. When the
beast stood on his hind legs to reach it, she flew over to
him and yanked the thorn from his paw.

The beast howled. But when he put his paw down, he understood what Fawn had done. With a grateful grunt, he went back to work.

Fawn was more curious than ever. She wanted to know everything about this strange creature!

Fawn rushed home to get her research tools, but Nyx
was there waiting for her.

"Did you hear that roar this morning?" Nyx asked.

Fawn pretended she hadn't.

"Listen, this thing might be a threat," said Nyx. "If you
find out what made that roar, I need to know."

"What will you do if you find it?" Fawn asked.

"My job," Nyx responded.

The next day, Fawn
returned to study the strange
creature. He ignored her for
most of the day, but, at sunset,
the glowing pixie dust that trailed
behind Fawn amazed the animal.
When Fawn sat down to make a note in her journal, the
beast nudged her. At last, they'd found a way to connect!
Fawn sprinkled pixie dust on a rock and placed it on his
rock pile. The creature was pleased. Exhausted, Fawn made
herself a bed of leaves and went to sleep.

It was dawn when the big animal nudged
Fawn awake. Behind the beast was a huge
horn-shaped tower made from rocks.

"Whoa," said Fawn. "Looks like somebody's
a night owl!"

Fawn wondered what the tower was for.
Suddenly, the beast picked her up with his tail
and plopped her on his head. Together they
marched into the forest.

"Where are we going?" asked Fawn.

The creature grumbled.
"Well, you don't have to be so gruff about it," Fawn said.
Then it hit her. "That's what I'll call you – Gruff!"

Gruff stopped at a clearing in the Summer Forest and set
Fawn down. He stomped the ground in a circle and then
dug out a rock. The process had begun again. This time,
Fawn turned it into a game. She used her pixie dust to lift
a rock from the ground, then Gruff knocked it into place on
the pile with his tail.

Next, Fawn lined up a row of rocks. But Gruff hit
them too hard. They sailed over the cliff towards
Sunflower Meadow!

Fawn shouted a warning to the garden fairies who
were working in the meadow.

Scout fairies rushed to the scene. "Is everyone accounted for?" asked Nyx.

"Yes, thanks to Fawn," answered a garden fairy. "If she hadn't shouted that warning we'd be flatter than a pumpkin seed."

"Fawn?" Nyx questioned.

Meanwhile, Fawn looked over the cliff and saw the scouts. "You have to get out of here," she told Gruff. But he was busy building.

Fawn did loops in front of him, pixie dust falling all around. "Okay, new game. It's called 'chase the fairy'!"

Finally, Gruff followed Fawn into the woods.

Nyx and the
scouts arrived at
the top of the cliff.
They examined
the pile of rocks.

Then, Nyx spotted a giant
trail of paw prints. The scouts
followed them into the woods.
Up ahead, the trees began
to shake and they heard branches
breaking. Whatever had made
those prints was close!

Gruff ran fast as he followed Fawn through
the forest, but the scouts flew faster. They threw
pouches of nightshade powder into the air in front
of Gruff and burst them open with arrows.

The nightshade drifted towards Gruff, but Fawn turned
sharply and the beast followed, avoiding the sleeping powder.
Nyx raced through the trees and stopped
at the edge of a cliff. Whatever they
had been chasing had disappeared!

Fawn decided that she wanted Gruff to meet her friends, so they could see he wasn't a monster.

"As you all know," she began. "I really learned my lesson about being smarter when it comes to dangerous animals. However...."

"Fawn, what's going on?" interrupted Tink.

"Ladies, say hello to Gruff!" The huge beast lowered himself from a tree branch.

"What is that?" gulped Rosetta.

"I don't actually know," admitted Fawn. "But I'm going to take him to the queen and show her that he's harmless."

Unfortunately, Nyx had reached the queen first. She had discovered that the comet had come before – 972 years ago – and with it had come the NeverBeast.

The NeverBeast had built four towers, one in each season of Pixie Hollow. Then, green storm clouds had formed and the monster had destroyed everything with lightning!

Just then, Gruff peeked in through the window. Fawn quickly distracted the queen. "How do we know this isn't just some crazy legend?"

"We've already located a tower in Summer," said Nyx. "This legend is real!"

Outside the window, pixie dust tickled
Gruff's nose. "ACHOO!"

Fawn pretended it was her that had sneezed.
"Whoa, I should get that checked," she said.

Queen Clarion looked outside. Luckily, she didn't see Gruff. The queen turned back to Fawn and Nyx and asked them to listen with their hearts and their heads. "I trust you both to do what's right for Pixie Hollow."

Fawn and her friends flew Gruff back to the forest. When they landed, Fawn explained what had happened.

"Nyx found this harebrained legend about a creature called the NeverBeast who shoots lightning to destroy Pixie Hollow," she said. "Nyx thinks Gruff is a monster. Crazy, right?"

"Even if you're right," said Tink, "it's not safe for him here."

Fawn took Gruff back to the second tower. Once he had finished it, the two sat together, gazing at the stars.

The next morning, the fairies in Pixie Hollow awoke to a worrying sight – thick, churning green clouds filled the sky. The scout fairies flew off towards the forest carrying a huge net.

Tinker Bell gasped. She knew they were going after Gruff.

Fawn had woken that morning to find that Gruff had gone. She asked Tink to help find him before the scouts did. They split up and Fawn saw that he had already built a tower in Autumn. So she flew into Winter. She saw the fourth and final tower, then spotted Tink on the ground. Gruff was looming over her.

"Tink!" Fawn cried, cradling Tinker Bell. "Gruff, what did you do?"

Gruff snarled and turned away. At that moment, lightning struck the tower! The air crackled with electricity.

As Fawn watched, Gruff transformed. Horns grew out of his head and a hump formed on his back. Just like the monster in the drawings!

Tink's friends took Tink to the healing fairy and huddled round her bed. But Fawn sat by herself. Again, she'd listened with her heart, not her head. Now, her best friend was hurt.

"Is she going to be okay?" Iridessa asked the healing fairy. The fairy nodded.

Everyone breathed a sigh of relief. "See, Fawn," Rosetta said, turning to face her. "She's going to be ..."

But Fawn had already left.

Fawn found Gruff sitting high on a ledge.
"Come here," she called. "I need to see you."
As soon as Gruff came into the open, the scout
fairies threw a net over him. The beast struggled
and groaned as the net was pulled tighter.
Fawn just watched, feeling guilty.

"Nightshade powder!" called Nyx. Five pouches exploded over Gruff, coating him. He fought to get free, then collapsed as the sleeping powder took effect.

"Mission accomplished!" shouted Nyx. "We captured the NeverBeast!"

Nyx turned to Fawn. "You did the right thing."

Fawn went to check on Tink. To her surprise, Tink was awake.

"I'm so sorry," said Fawn.

"There's nothing to be sorry for," Tink replied. "Gruff is exactly who you said he was."

Tink explained that lightning had split a tree right next to her. Gruff had pushed her out of the way just in time. He'd saved her life!

"And I betrayed him!" cried Fawn. Then, she ran for the door.

"Where are you going?" asked Tink.

"To do the right thing," Fawn replied.

Tinker Bell quickly fetched the other fairies. They followed Fawn through the growing storm and set Gruff free.

Gruff's vision was blurry from the nightshade, so Fawn used the glow from her pixie dust to lead him to the first tower. There, lightning arced off the rocks onto Gruff. Waves of electricity surged across his body. The girls watched in awe as huge wings grew out of his back!

Fawn now understood Gruff's purpose. "He's not here to shoot lightning at Pixie Hollow," she said. "He's here to draw it away!"

Gruff stomped on the ground.

"I understand," Fawn told him. "We're going to the other towers. Follow my glow!"

Fawn led Gruff through
the forest to the Autumn tower.
The rocks were brightly lit from
a constant stream of lightning.
Gruff charged at the tower and the lightning
jumped onto his horns instead. Then, the tower
crumbled and the lightning cleared from the area.
    Fairies on the ground watched in amazement as
Gruff flew overhead, led by Fawn. At the Winter tower,
lightning again leaped on to Gruff.
    "One more to go!" shouted Fawn.

Fawn and Gruff had just reached the final tower when Nyx knocked it down! Gruff fell to the ground.

The lightning that had been focused on Gruff's horns split into hundreds of smaller high-voltage bolts! Lightning was everywhere in Pixie Hollow, hitting the ground and setting trees on fire.

"Nyx!" cried Fawn. "What are you doing?"

"Saving Pixie Hollow," Nyx yelled.

Suddenly, a bolt of lightning flashed
towards Nyx, but Gruff blocked it and
absorbed the strike.
    "Don't you get it, Nyx?" screamed Fawn.
"He was saving Pixie Hollow!"

Gruff tried to rebuild the tower.

"It's too late," said Fawn. The swirling clouds pulsed with electricity. "How can we catch it all?"

Suddenly, Fawn realized all of the lightning was coming from the eye of the storm.

She and Gruff looked at each other. Both knew what had to be done.

"Follow me," said Fawn.

Gruff followed Fawn's glow as they flew up to the centre of the storm. As they got closer, Gruff pushed Fawn behind him.

Lightning came from every direction, drawn to the beast's horns. Gruff gathered up all the storm's energy until the clouds were drained.

Then, in one enormous blast – BOOOOM! – Gruff shook off the energy, sending waves of heat and light far out over the sea.

The storm was over. Fairies flew into the sky and used pixie dust to catch Fawn and Gruff as they fell to the ground.

Gruff, with scorched fur, was all right but Fawn was motionless. The beast leaned over and nuzzled her cheek. As he did, one tiny last bit of electrical energy sparked onto Fawn. Moments later, her eyes fluttered open. "Hey, there's my big furry monster," she said.

Everyone cheered!

Before long, Gruff and Fawn had made a full recovery. Gruff was a hero. "They finally see what I see," Fawn said to him.

Gruff helped repair the damage from the storm, but he soon started to tire. Fawn listened to his heart and heard that it was slowing down – that meant it was time for him to go back into hibernation.

"How long are we talking about?" asked Rosetta.

Fawn held back her tears. "About a thousand years."

The girls understood what that meant.

"We'll never see him again," said Tink.

Fawn and the girls led Gruff back to his cave. Hundreds of fairies lined the route to wish him well. Gruff could hardly believe it.

Nyx told Gruff she had a gift for him. "The enduring respect of a grateful scout," she said.

Fawn kissed Gruff on the nose. "Hey, big guy," she said sweetly. "I won't see you again. But I know you'll always be there when we need you."

Gruff settled into his bed and smiled.

"I'm really going to miss you," Fawn whispered. "I love you, Gruff."

And with that, Gruff's eyes closed and he drifted off to sleep.